P9-BXY-873

FIRST DAY
JITTERS

ini Charlesbridge

FIRST DAY
JITTERS

JULIE DANNEBERG

ILLUSTRATED BY JUDY LOVE

To Jack and Buddie—J.D.

For Matthew, who never gets "first day jitters,"
but willingly posed for me anyway, with love—J.L.

YOUTH SERVICES
Falmouth Public Library
300 Main Street
Falmouth, MA 02540
508-457-2555

Text copyright © 2000 by Julie Danneberg
Illustrations copyright © 2000 by Judy Love
All rights reserved, including the right of reproduction in whole or in part in any form.
Charlesbridge and colophon are registered trademarks of Charlesbridge Publishing, Inc.

At the time of publication, all URLs printed in this book were accurate and active. Charlesbridge,
the author, and the illustrator are not responsible for the content or accessibility of any website.

Published by Charlesbridge, 9 Galen Street, Watertown, MA 02472
(617) 926-0329 • www.charlesbridge.com

Library of Congress Cataloging-in-Publication Data
Danneberg, Julie, 1958–
First day jitters / Julie Danneberg; illustrated by Judy Love.
p. cm.
Summary: Sarah is afraid to start at a new school, but both she and
the reader are in for a surprise when she gets to her class.
ISBN 978-1-58089-054-0 (reinforced for library use)
ISBN 978-1-58089-061-8 (softcover)
ISBN 978-1-60734-549-7 (ebook)
[1. First day of school—Fiction. 2. Schools—Fiction. 3. Teachers—Fiction.]
I. Love, Judith DuFour, ill. II. Title.
PZ7.D2327 Fi 2000
[E]—dc21   99-050095

Printed in China
(hc) 25 24 23 22 21 20
(pb) 47 46 45 44 43

Illustrations done in ink and watercolors on 100% Rag Strathmore Bristol Vellum
Display type and text type set in LunchBox and Electra
Printed by 1010 Printing International Limited in Huizhou, Guangdong, China
Cover design by Sara Gillingham; interior design by Diane M. Earley
Production supervision by Brian G. Walker

"Sarah, dear, time to get out of bed," Mr. Hartwell said, poking his head through the bedroom doorway. "You don't want to miss the first day at your new school do you?"

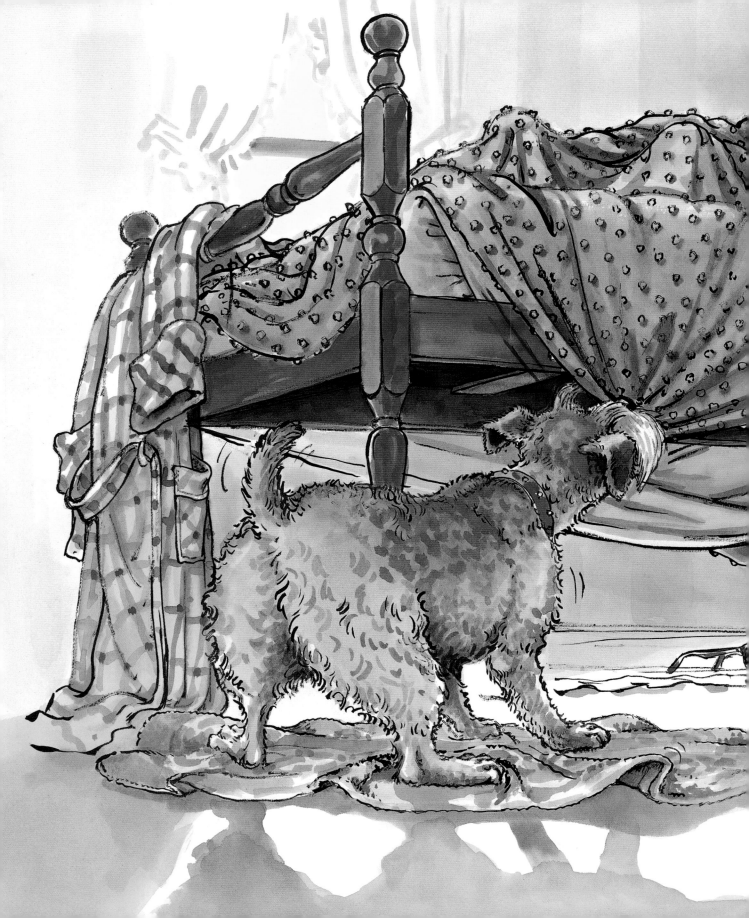

"I'm not going," said Sarah, and pulled the covers over her head.

"Of course you're going, honey," said Mr. Hartwell, as he walked over to the window and snapped up the shade.

"No, I'm not. I don't want to start over again. I hate my new school," Sarah said. She tunneled down to the end of her bed.

"How can you hate your new school, sweetheart?"
Mr. Hartwell chuckled. "You've never been there
before! Don't worry. You liked your other school,
you'll like this one. Besides, just think of all the new
friends you'll meet."

"That's just it. I don't know anybody, and it will be hard, and...I just hate it, that's all."

"What will everyone think if you aren't there?
We told them you were coming!"

"They will think that I am lucky and they will wish that they were at home in bed like me."

Mr. Hartwell sighed. "Sarah Jane Hartwell, I'm not playing this silly game one second longer. I'll see you downstairs in five minutes."

Sarah tumbled out of bed.

She stumbled into the bathroom.

She fumbled into her clothes.

"My head hurts," she moaned as she trudged into the kitchen.

Mr. Hartwell handed Sarah a piece of toast and her lunchbox.

They walked to the car. Sarah's
hands were cold and clammy.

They drove down the street.
She couldn't breathe.

And then they were there.
"I feel sick," said Sarah
weakly.
"Nonsense," said Mr.
Hartwell. "You'll love your
new school once you
get started. Oh, look.
There's your principal,
Mrs. Burton."
Sarah slumped down
in her seat.

"Oh, Sarah," Mrs. Burton gushed, peeking into the car. "There you are. Come on. I'll show you where to go."

She led Sarah into the building and walked quickly through the crowded hallways. "Don't worry. Everyone is nervous the first day," she said over her shoulder as Sarah rushed to keep up.

When they got to
the classroom, most
of the children were
already in their seats.

The class looked up as Mrs. Burton cleared her throat.

"Class. Class. Attention, please," said Mrs. Burton.

When the class was quiet she led Sarah to the front of the room and said, "Class, I would like you to meet...

...your new teacher, Mrs. Sarah Jane Hartwell."